# BARCELONA AWAY

# BARCELONA AWAY

## TOM PALMER

First published in Great Britain in 2012

Diffusion
*an imprint of*
SPCK
36 Causton Street
London SW1P 4ST
www.spckpublishing.co.uk

Reprinted with amendments 2014

ISBN 978-1-908713-01-8

Typeset by Graphicraft Ltd, Hong Kong
First printed in Great Britain by MPG Books
Subsequently digitally reprinted in Great Britain

Produced on paper from sustainable forests

# Contents

———◆•●•◆———

# 1

## *The Outlaws*

---

Saturday evening and Matt was at his in-laws.

Whenever they visited the in-laws, they ended up playing board games.

Matt hated board games.

There were five people round the table. Matt and his daughter, Grace, on one side. Matt's wife, Sarah, and her parents on the other.

Out of all the board games in his father-in-law's collection, Matt hated this one more than any other. It was one of those quiz games that was about showing how much you knew.

That made Matt feel tense.

If it had been up to Matt, they would all have been watching the live match on Sky. But he knew it wasn't worth suggesting that. This was a family occasion. Football was not on the agenda.

*What is the point of having Sky Sports, if you didn't have it on all the time?* Matt thought to himself.

He would never get to the bottom of that.

The evening wore on.

And on.

Matt was just about coping with his mother-in-law.

She had already asked him how his construction job was going.

She had brought him a beer.

Two things that made him feel good.

It might be a rubbish brand of beer, but it was the thought that counted. And Matt was pretty sure she didn't serve rubbish beers just to annoy him.

The old man was a different case. Matt could easily imagine his father-in-law at the supermarket buying beer that he knew would annoy his son-in-law. Just to irritate him.

The board game had started well. Matt had whispered the right answer to his daughter several times. Matt and Grace were a great team.

But now things had started changing. The Outlaws were on a run, getting question after question right.

'It's slipping through your fingers, Matthew,' said his father-in-law, rubbing his bald head.

Matt pretended to smile, his arm tight around Grace. He felt his daughter stiffen. She was as competitive as he was.

'In fact,' the old man went on, 'I think you've blown it.'

Matt could feel the anger rising in him now. He knew his neck would be going red. If he could just focus on the game and not let his father-in-law get to him.

Matt rolled the dice and Grace moved the counter.

'Sport,' said his father-in-law, looking at where the counter had landed. 'You should get this, Matthew. You think you know *everything* about sport.'

'Dad!' said Matt's wife, Sarah.

She was warning her father off.

'Your wife's defending you, Matthew,' said the old man, winking.

Matt was really angry now. He hated this banter that he couldn't respond to. He hated being called Matthew. He was hot around his eyes. His head was thumping.

And the worst thing was, he knew Grace had sensed it. She was looking up at him, checking to make sure he was happy. He noticed that she had tucked her straight brown hair behind her ears, just like Sarah did.

Matt gently kissed the top of his daughter's head to put her at ease. She smiled back at him.

'Ready for your question, Matthew?'

*Ready to smash your face in the next time you call me Matthew!* Matt thought, aware that everyone's eyes were on him.

His wife.

His daughter.

The in-laws.

'How many Scottish Championships did Alex Ferguson win with Aberdeen?'

Grace looked up at Matt.

His father-in-law went on. 'It's one, two, three or four.'

Matt understood that this was a key point in the game. If they got this right, then they'd be close to winning. If they got it wrong, it would open up the win for the in-laws.

And that was the last thing that Matt wanted.

**What do you think?**

What do you think of Matt's father-in-law?

Why doesn't Matt get on with him?

If he finds it so hard, why does he agree to spend time with his in-laws?

# 2

## *The soap dispenser*

---

Matt patted his daughter on the arm. He knew the answer to the quiz question.

How many Scottish Championships did Alex Ferguson win with Aberdeen?

Two.

'Say two,' he whispered to Grace.

Grace smiled triumphantly at her grandad. 'Two,' she announced.

Grandad smirked. 'Are you sure?' he asked.

Grace looked at Matt again, questioning. Matt nodded. It *was* two. He knew it was two. The old man was just teasing Grace.

'Say two,' he said again.

'Two,' said Grace.

But Grandad was shaking his head. 'Three,' he said, a laugh rising in his voice.

Matt stood up, gently slipping his arm from around his daughter.

He had to get out of the room.

Now.

Right now.

'Toilet,' he coughed, then headed out of the door and upstairs without looking round.

This was the only way.

As he walked up the stairs he muttered a different swear word each time his foot hit a step.

Damn.

Damn.

Damn.

Damn.

His face was on fire. He could barely see.

Then Matt heard his father-in-law laughing.

For a second he stopped on the stairs. He felt an irresistible urge to go back into the sitting room and launch himself at his father-in-law. Finish him off. This was doing his head in.

Somehow, though, Matt managed to keep his hand on the banister and not go down. He worked his way up instead, gently shut the bathroom door and fell on his knees.

This was the last time, the *last* time he was coming here.

He closed his eyes and put his forehead on the side of the bath.

*Keep it in*, he told himself. *Keep it inside.*

He took deep breaths, counted to twenty, thought of things that made him feel happy, like his daughter's cuddles, like his wife's smile, like smashing Grandad's face in.

More breathing.

Deep, deep breathing.

More slow counting.

One . . . two . . . three . . . four . . .

After a minute or two Matt felt calmer. He knew he would have to go back downstairs. He owed it to Sarah and Grace. And he felt proud he'd kept the anger in.

Before going down Matt pissed and flushed the toilet.

Then he went to wash his hands.

The soap situation at the Outlaws was pretty unusual. They used a posh soap called Imperial Leather. There was a little plastic arm that came away from the tiles at the back of the sink, with a magnet on the end of it. Matt's mother-in-law would slip a small piece of metal into the top of the bar of soap, meaning the soap would stick magnetically to the little plastic arm.

'Soap can get messy,' Matt could remember his mother-in-law saying. 'There's no need for messy soap.'

Matt did not like the soap magnet.

After washing his hands, he tried to put the soap back on it. But, as often happened, the soap wouldn't stay up there.

He tried three times.

No luck.

He rinsed the soap, hoping that would help.

Still no luck.

So, Matt took the plastic soap arm in both his hands and ripped it off the wall. Then he threw it hard against the floor and repeatedly stamped on it two-footed, until he heard the noise of banging on the bathroom door.

**What do you think?**

Why does Matt think it's right to try to 'keep it inside'?

Why do you think he loses it with the soap?

How do you think his in-laws will react to the mess he's made?

# 3

## In the pub

———•◦•———

'So how did you get out of that?' asked Fenn, laughing at Matt's story about his in-laws.

Fenn was tall and muscular, with very short hair. He was the lads' unofficial leader, making all the plans, arranging whatever needed arranging. Whatever Fenn asked, people did.

'I had to make something up,' shouted Matt above the noise of the adverts on the big screen.

Matt and his mates were in the pub. Fenn. Sicky. Andy. And the rest.

It was just before four on Sunday afternoon, Arsenal v. Man U on the big screen. He felt warm in the pub and there was a comforting smell of beer. Someone was smoking in the doorway, the delicious whiff of cigarette smoke wafting back in. Matt was on his third pint of Stella and was feeling good.

'Like what?' Fenn pushed him. 'There was a burglar? You had to defend yourself with a soap dispenser against a psycho?'

Matt laughed. Fenn was being funny, so now everyone was looking at them, hoping for a good story during the adverts and before the game kicked off.

So Matt delivered.

'I heard someone at the bathroom door. Bloody Grandad, of course. He was shouting. "What the bloody hell's going on in there?" And I had to think quick. So I grabbed the soap thing and gashed my hand with it.'

Matt held up his bandaged hand, then went on, the others nodding like it was a normal thing to do.

'I hit a lovely vein – 'cos the blood was pouring out. Then I ripped up this piece of loose lino on the bathroom floor that the old man has been saying he'd fix for ages and went down into the hall, going, "Argghhh, my hand. I tripped up." Everyone was in the hall by now. And the mother-in-law was laying into the old man before he got a word in. "I've told you a hundred times to get that lino sorted. That's what the poor lad's tripped over, isn't it, Matt?"'

Matt grinned. 'I just had to nod once. And Grandad is backing down the hall, the smile wiped right off his face.'

'Result!' Andy said.

Fenn, Andy and Sicky were laughing now. But then the music started on the big screen, taking everyone's attention. Everyone was booing as the camera focused on Wayne Rooney running on to the pitch.

Matt leapt up, feeling excited about the match and his story and the beer that was making him feel just right.

He shouted, 'Get off the pitch, Rooney, you fat idiot, you bald git.' His voice disappeared into dozens of men shouting abuse at a man in a red shirt.

At half-time, there was business to attend to.

Everyone went quiet. The barman even turned the sound down.

Matt rubbed his hands together. He and everybody knew what this was about. It was time to sort out the plans for Turkey.

Fenn stood up. 'Right,' he said. 'The flight is at ten in the morning from Manchester. We need to get to the airport by half eight, so

I'll pick you all up outside the pub at seven.
OK?'

Fenn had a work van that you could fit fifteen
lads in without much trouble, if he cleared out
all the tools.

Matt nodded, along with Sicky and Andy.

'Don't be late,' said Fenn. 'If you are you can
walk to Turkey.'

'We'll be there,' said Andy.

'I'll keep the tickets,' Fenn went on. 'But you
need to bring what?'

'Passport,' said Sicky.

'Beer money,' added Andy.

'Tourist guide to museums of interest in
Istanbul,' Matt said, keeping a straight face.

'What?' said Sicky, thinking Matt meant it.

'More bloody beer money,' shouted Matt,
shoving Sicky, so that his beer spilled.

Andy led the laughing. Laughing at Sicky's expense.

'Like Matt would want to go to a museum or
read a guidebook, Sicky,' Andy said.

Matt saw Sicky's face cloud over. But it was
nothing to worry about. Sicky could be moody,
but he was a lightweight.

In fact, Matt didn't really like Sicky. He was one of those lads who was always trying to make himself look better than everyone else. Always trying to be best mates with Fenn at Matt's expense.

Matt ignored Sicky most of the time, but Sicky still annoyed him. Sicky was short and wiry, like a stupid little dog. And Matt knew that one of these days they'd have a run-in and that he'd have to be sharp to get the better of the younger man.

**What do you think?**

What do you think about Matt's excuse?

How did it make his father-in-law feel?

What does Matt like about the pub?

# 4

## *Give me George in my heart*

'Matt,' said Fenn, 'you've been to Istanbul. What's it like?'

It was the adverts again, the second half about to kick off. Everyone had sorted out a drink. The smokers were coming in. Only three lads were standing outside, visible through the window, wolfing down burgers from the McDonald's down the road.

'All right,' Matt said, remembering a trip him and Sarah had made to Turkey before Grace was born. Beaches. Boat trips up the river. Museums even.

'Pubs?' Fenn asked. 'Any good?'

'Not bad,' Matt replied. 'Little bars hidden away up alleys. Or you can sit out in the squares and that. Should be sunny. Warmer than it is here, anyway.'

'What about English bars?' Andy asked. 'Can you get decent beer, or is it all Turkish shit?'

'Turkish bars mostly,' Matt said.

'No way,' Sicky cut in. 'So no chance of getting some decent English beer. Is it all Turkish crap?'

'It's Turkey, Sicky, you muppet. It's gonna be Turkish bars and Turkish beer.'

'But what's Turkish beer like? Is it like our beer?'

'It's beer,' Matt shouted, now the volume was up on the big screen again. 'What more do you want?'

Fenn and Andy were laughing again. Laughing with Matt.

'Your round, Sick?' Fenn asked. But, really, it was an order, not a question.

Sicky frowned. 'Same again?' he asked, putting his hand into his pocket.

Everyone nodded.

Matt smiled as he watched Sicky pushing into the half-time scrum at the bar.

He turned his mind to Turkey. Matt felt really excited about this trip. A group of them went to a couple of European away games every season. One in the group stages. One in the knockouts. Last season they'd done Milan and Moscow.

Win or lose, it was always a good day out. Twenty-four hours of drinking and football and banter. No work. No worries. No stress. No soap dispensers.

Just fun.

And beer.

And more beer.

When Sicky got back from the bar there was an advert for a forthcoming England game on the TV. Some of the lads were singing England songs.

'*Eng-er-land! Eng-er-land! Eng-er-land!*'

Matt took a huge drink of his Stella, then started another chant. The singing and the beer had got him in the mood. He shouted at the top of his voice.

'*Give me George in my heart, keep me English.*'

Immediately he had five, then ten, voices joining in, the noise bouncing off the walls of the pub.

'*Give me George in my heart, I pray.*'

There was nothing like the feeling of starting a chant. At the pub. At the match. It was always the same. It made you feel powerful.

'*Give me George in my heart, keep me English.*
*Keep me English till my dying day.*'

The pub shook to the sound of the singing. And Matt sat back and beamed.

He wished that they were on the plane to Turkey already.

**What do you think?**

What do you think about what Turkey has to offer?

Do you think the others are fair to Sicky?

Why does the chant make Matt feel powerful?

# 5

## *Bedtime*

———◆◦◆———

As darkness was falling on Monday night, Matt glanced at the clock, then at Grace, who was telling a story with the dolls around her dolls' house. Her dark hair had been plaited. Not by Matt, though. By Sarah.

'Bedtime, sweetie,' said Matt.

'Not yet. Please, Daddy. Five more minutes.'

Matt shook his head. He knew he had to be firm at bedtime. Sarah always was.

'Come on,' he said. 'If we brush your teeth quickly we'll have time to read that book we got you from the library.'

On Saturday, before the trip to the in-laws, Matt and Grace had visited the public library. Grace had been asking questions about Matt's trip to watch football in Turkey, so they had gone to find a book about the country.

Matt often did this with Grace. They would read from a book that was something to do with what was going on in the family. Like a place they were going to on holiday, something Grace had seen on TV, or a subject that Grace was doing at school.

Matt loved reading with Grace. He'd sit on her bed once he'd tucked her in, and they'd take it in turns reading together. It was probably the time he felt most calm and happy. Just the two of them.

They talked about the Turkish flag – a star and a crescent moon on a red background.

They looked at a map and found out the names of the seas and mountains in Turkey. They found pictures of amazing birds and animals that lived in the wild areas.

Then they found a page in the book that was about St George.

'But I thought St George was *our* patron saint,' frowned Grace.

'So did I,' agreed Matt.

'How can he be our patron saint if he was Turkish?'

Grace had asked a good question and Matt was struggling with it. The song he'd been singing in the pub the day before came into his head, but he quickly put the thought away.

'I thought he fought dragons in England,' Grace went on.

Matt glanced at the clock. He should be switching the light out now.

But he also knew that he had to take questions like this from Grace seriously and help her find out the answer. If he just brushed it away, without answering her, she might stop asking him questions. And he knew that every child should be encouraged to ask questions, to want to find out.

'Well, he did,' Matt replied, trying to work out exactly what to say. 'And he is a really important part of our history.' Matt smiled. 'Maybe he thought Turkey was rubbish, so he came over here and killed all the dragons.'

'Hmmm,' answered Grace.

'No?'

'No. I think our patron saint should be English. Not Turkish. That's stupid. I think we should have a new patron saint.'

'Who would you like it to be?' asked Matt, genuinely interested in who his daughter thought could be the patron saint of England.

Names were flashing through his mind. Great English people he could suggest to her. Like Lord Nelson and the Duke of Wellington. He thought of Florence Nightingale too. He wanted to suggest a woman to his daughter. He wanted her to understand that women were just as important as men.

But Grace came up with an idea first.

'I think it should be you, Daddy,' she smiled.

Matt felt tears prickling in his eyes. He hugged his daughter.

Sometimes he thought he could burst with the feelings of love he had for her.

'You're the best,' Matt told her. 'If you carry on being such a lovely and thoughtful girl all your life, *you'll* be the patron saint of England, no question.'

When Grace was asleep, Matt pulled the duvet over her shoulders and looked down at her. She looked so peaceful and happy. He bent down and kissed her forehead, then walked slowly out of the room, pulling the door to.

**What do you think?**

In what ways is Matt a good dad?

Why does he enjoy reading with Grace?

In what ways is he different with Grace from how he is with his mates?

Does it matter that St George wasn't English?

# 6

## *Departures*

---

There was only time for four drinks in the departure lounge.

Matt had a couple of bottles of Stella, then two triple malts. He knew that if he drank pints he'd be going to the toilet on the plane all the time, so he went for the sensible option.

Nine o'clock in the morning.

The bar was in the middle of the departure lounge. Hundreds of people were milling around it, leaving for New York, Dubai and dozens of other destinations.

None of the lads were wearing colours. But you could see them everywhere.

A large group of them were standing round a sleek, banana-yellow sports car parked up outside WH Smith. Two spectacular girls in short skirts were handing out leaflets. Matt had already been over there to find out what was going on.

It was a raffle. For the car. Tickets cost £25 each.

And people were actually paying.

Matt grinned. Half-pissed men on their way to the football, plus good-looking girls in short skirts, plus a fancy car. It was a winner. He wished he'd thought of it.

But as well as the other lads from the football all over the airport, there were normal people there too. People who were not going to the football.

Men in suits.

Groups of young women.

Families with pushchairs and parents holding the hands of toddlers.

Seeing men with children inspired Matt to have a look round the duty free shop to get something for Grace, but he knew that it was best to get something on the way back. He'd only lose something if he bought it now.

You never knew what would happen on one of these trips, so it was best to play it safe.

Matt was finding it hard to relax, waiting around in the airport.

Maybe it was because of the vast expanses of white wall and huge windows, then the miles of concrete outside the windows.

Or maybe it was the fact that he was with the football lads, but they couldn't really behave like they were at the football yet.

He wanted to raise his voice, get into the mood, have some fun, but there were too many people around. So when Fenn suggested to him and Andy that they go to the toilet before their flight was called, Matt took his chance.

As soon as they were in the toilet, away from the crowds, he started up his chant again.

*'Give me George in my heart, keep me English . . .'*

It sounded good in the toilet. Great acoustics. Great, too, that Andy was joining in. They took a cubicle each and hammered it out, full blast.

*'Give me George in my heart, I pray.*

*Give me George in my heart, keep me English.*

*Keep me English till my dying day.'*

Matt zipped up his fly and headed out of his cubicle. He was belting it out now.

*'No surrender, no surrender . . .'*

Matt stopped because he was face to face with a large man in a suit.

The man was looking at him in a funny way. The kind of way that meant he didn't like what Matt was saying.

Matt could hear the loud voices of Fenn and Andy finishing the song.

The man was still staring at him with a look of disgust.

'What are you looking at?' Matt barked at the man.

The man looked like he was about to say what he thought of Matt, but now Fenn and Andy were out of their cubicles and standing either side of him.

That made the man take a step backwards.

Fenn stepped forward. Andy too.

'Come on,' Andy said. 'Let's have you.'

Then the man was gone, leaving the three friends alone in the toilets.

'Don't think he liked your singing voice, Matty,' said Fenn.

Matt shook his head.

'No taste,' he said. 'No taste.'

**What do you think?**

Why is Matt so excited?

How do you think the man in the toilet felt?

Do you think that Matt would have behaved
differently if Grace had been with him?

# 7

## *Flying*

---

On the flight everyone was quieter.

They were on a warning.

The captain had come out of his cockpit before the plane took off, flanked by two air stewards, one male and one female. He told them that everyone was welcome on board. But he also said that he had piloted football fans before and he had some special rules.

Two rules.

Rule one: there would be no alcohol on sale on the flight.

Rule two: if there was any over-excitement, he'd turn the plane round and head back to England.

*Over-excitement.* That was how he'd put it.

Matt knew what the pilot meant. For the next four hours they had to be sensible.

He looked around the plane. He tried not to think about the fact that this was just a thin tube of metal, stuck to a couple of flaps, that was about to be hurled thirty thousand feet into the air for four hours.

Matt always had thoughts like that in planes.

It was better to think about football.

He glanced behind him to see Andy. He was glad that Andy was a couple of rows back. If anyone was going to cause trouble it was Andy. He had this way about him. If someone said, 'Don't do this,' Andy would try to do it. If anyone was going to hit the man in the toilets, it would have been Andy.

Matt was sitting with Fenn and Sicky.

'I was reading this book with our Grace,' Matt said to Fenn, who was by the window over the wing. This was Matt's attempt at being sensible.

'Well done, mate,' said Fenn. 'Was she helping you spell out the words?'

Sicky laughed loudly, but Matt went on.

'About Turkey,' he said. 'Did you know that St George was Turkish?'

'Yeah?'

'Yeah,' said Matt.

'I wish we could get a drink,' Sicky interrupted.

'Mmmm,' said Fenn, smirking. 'But you can understand why they don't want drinking. I mean, we don't want any singing on the flight, do we?'

Sicky started it.

Under his breath.

Quiet at first.

'*Give me George in my heart, keep me English.*'

The three friends were giggling now as more voices began to join in. Nobody seemed bothered that St George was Turkish.

'*Give me George in my heart, I pray.*'

Matt bent over and covered his face. He was laughing so much he could hardly join in. It was that kind of uncontrollable laughing you did with your mates when you were ten or eleven.

'*Give me George in my heart, keep me English . . .*'

The male steward was next to them within seconds.

Matt looked up and smiled.

The steward was looking directly at him. 'Excuse me, sir, please will you stop chanting?'

Matt flushed red and stopped laughing.

'Yeah, Matt,' said Sicky. 'Stop chanting.'

Matt straightened up and tried to look unflustered. But inside he was furious.

Who the hell was this man to come and tell him to shut up?

And what was a man doing being an air hostess anyway?

Matt's mouth was hurting as he ground his teeth hard.

He looked at the steward and remembered the captain's warning.

He was quite sure the pilot would turn the plane round if he had a good reason to. There was no way Matt was going to risk that.

'Sorry,' he muttered, glaring at the steward with the darkest, most violent look he could muster.

**What do you think?**

Why does the captain have rules on the flight?

Why does Sicky start the chant?

Why is Matt furious?

# 8

## *You're shit and you know you are*

———◆◆◆———

From the moment the Turkish team scored their first goal, Matt felt bad.

After ten minutes of being one up, the home fans were still so noisy that any chants from the away fans were easily drowned out. And the English players looked like they didn't care they were losing.

Matt scowled.

Rubbish. This was rubbish.

When the second goal went in, the game was over. Matt turned to look away from the pitch. The home fans had lit flares and they were waving them, the bright lights burning the backs of Matt's eyes.

*Damn it*, Matt thought. If English fans lit flares they'd be banned for life. How come bloody Turks were allowed to do it? Why did English fans always get the rough end of the stick?

The match went on.

And on.

Still a wall of noise from the home fans. Nothing from the away fans.

Sickening.

Matt inspected his fingernails. How long until the final whistle?

When the third goal went in Andy lost it.

'You idiots! Get your bloody fingers out. This lot are a third world country and they're beating us. For Christ's sake! We should be slaughtering them.'

He was shouting. Or screaming. His voice was breaking, he was so furious.

A heavy smoke drifted across the away end. From the flares.

And with the smoke, came a song.

*'You're sheet and you know you are.*

*You're sheet and you know you are . . .'*

That was when Andy really lost it. And Matt could understand why. He felt the same.

There was only one thing worse than being taunted by foreign opposition fans after you'd travelled hundreds of miles. And that was being taunted by them in your own language.

Matt watched Andy turn and start to jerk at something near his feet. Seconds later he had a yellow plastic seat in his hands. He lifted it above his head and hurled it on to the pitch.

And then everyone was doing it.

The snaps and cracks of seats being ripped out.

The shower of seats skimming on to the pitch.

Then Andy was walking down the concrete steps, waving his arms around.

'Come on!' Andy shouted. 'Come on! Let's sort this out.'

And just as he did, the final whistle blew.

Several lads left quickly now.

Fenn caught Matt's eye, nodding. That meant it was time to go.

Matt felt Sicky, behind him, push him along the row, towards the steps, after Andy.

It was obvious what was going to happen now.

**What do you think?**

Why does Matt think that English fans 'get the rough end of the stick'? Is he right?

Why does Matt want the match to end?

What do you think of the way Andy behaves? Should his friends have tried to stop him?

# 9

## *Revenge*

---

A mass of English fans stormed down the steps, through a tunnel and out of the football stand.

They were not happy.

It was hard enough losing and your team playing like idiots, but to hear the home supporters taunting them was too much. And taunting them in English.

*'You're shit and you know you are.'*

Over and over again.

Fenn was alongside Matt, Sicky behind, as they marched out of the stadium towards the town centre. Police stood on either side of the road, slapping batons against their leather gloves. Andy was in the leading group.

Nobody said a word as they all headed into town. None of them looked at the police or each other.

But Matt knew what was coming. It helped him with his anger. He could keep the rage inside because he knew he was about to get the chance to use it.

Everyone around them knew what was coming. Two or three hundred lads, mingling with the ordinary fans, the ones wearing club colours, the ones who wanted a quiet beer before getting their flight home.

For Matt and his friends there would be no quiet beer. They had other things to do and two hours before the coaches would come for them.

That was plenty of time.

When they were nearly in the centre of town, the fans had thinned out, heading down the quiet alleys that led to the main square.

Soon.

Matt could tell it was going to be soon.

He could feel all the anger melting away. His frown and gritted teeth were relaxing. He began to smile. He was feeling good.

And now the lads ahead of them were running. So Matt ran too, rushing past other familiar faces, wanting to be at the front.

As he ran he thought about the steward on the flight and the fans goading him at the final whistle.

This was for them. This was for them and every other Turk that got in their way.

They burst out into the main square running. Over a hundred of them. The first café was on the right. Even before Matt got there, he could see chairs flying and people running for cover.

He sprinted to the heart of the action, picked up a heavy wooden chair and hurled it at the café entrance. Then, not watching to see its impact, he grabbed a table and rammed it into a pair of small trees in plant pots, scattering them.

Matt could hear screaming and shouting around him. He could smell meat and burning and metal. Above him more English fans had found a way up on to a balcony, where they had torn down a Turkish flag and were setting fire to it.

Matt picked up a second chair, but before he threw it, he sensed a change was coming. Another, deeper noise.

Matt looked over his shoulder.

Men.

Two dozen Turkish men, running towards them, gesturing to the flag-burners.

Matt knew his job.

He turned his attention from attacking the café to defending it.

Him and fifty others.

As the Turkish men came on, chairs and bottles and glasses rained down on them. Matt saw his chair hit one man, knocking him down. He shouted a loud war cry, then picked up a second chair to take out another Turk.

Glancing behind him, he saw that the café was on fire now.

As Matt moved and did what he needed to do, he realized that he had never felt as good as this.

He was strong.

He was brave.

He was happy.

But he had to keep going. They all did. No thinking.

More Turkish men were coming now.

Time to act.

In the chaos Matt saw blades flashing in the light coming from the flames. He heard a bang.

A shot? Was it a gunshot?

And sirens.

The police. Or worse, the army.

The fifty were scattering now, back up the alley. Only twenty left, with no sign of Sicky and Fenn.

It felt different this time.

No sense of being in control. Something darker.

Matt knew it was time to leave.

He dropped the chair he was about to throw and turned to run.

But as he ran towards the alley they had come down, out of the corner of his eye he saw something out of place.

A man on the ground.

**What do you think?**

Does Matt really enjoy football, or something else?

How would things have been different if Matt's team had won?

Matt thinks that knowing what was coming 'helped him with his anger'. What do you think?

How do you think the owner of the café will feel?

# 10

## *Rumours*

It was quiet at the airport. Too quiet.

Normally, even if they'd lost, there was banter, laughter, messing around.

But not tonight.

Tonight there were just hundreds of men. Mostly men. All sitting around under the bright white lights and between the featureless white walls of the airport, saying very little.

Matt had caught a taxi to the airport with a couple of lads he knew from the pubs back home. It was the safest option. He knew he had to get out of that dark labyrinth of a city centre. There were shadows everywhere, like ghosts.

Now Matt was sitting alone in the departure lounge. He'd been through security. He'd bought a coffee. But it was weird foreign coffee, and he wasn't sure he liked its bitter taste.

He felt tired, but he knew he wouldn't be able to sleep.

He felt hungry, but he didn't want to eat.

He stared, back through security, at lines of English football fans holding their passports. Silent. Sullen. Behind them were a couple of TV camera crews. Bright lights and microphones were being thrust in people's faces.

Matt closed his eyes.

In the silence, it was easy to pick up the sound of the one man talking. He was having a conversation on the phone.

'He was dead. I'm telling you, he was dead.'

A pause.

'I saw the ambulance come. They checked his pulse, tried that CPR thing, then just dumped his body in the back of the ambulance.'

A second pause.

'I don't know. It could be anyone.'

Matt felt sick.

He thought about the man he'd seen on the floor. Was he the dead one? Was someone really dead?

Then he thought about the TV cameras and the microphones outside.

And it hit him like a ten-ton truck.

Grace.

Sarah.

What if they switched on the TV and saw the lines of men at the airport?

What if they heard that someone was dead?

Would they be searching through the crowds of football fans still alive to find Matt's face?

Might they think that he was dead?

No. Not that.

He couldn't bear that.

Matt pulled his mobile phone out of his pocket. To call home. It didn't matter if it cost hundreds of pounds. He had to talk to them, tell them he was safe.

He dialled.

But it wouldn't ring.

He dialled again.

Now all he could hear was a voice.

A Turkish voice.

*'Jabber jabber jabber jabber. Blah blah blah.'*

Come on!

Matt kept trying, but it was impossible. So he went over to a pay phone and shoved his credit card into it.

He dialled.

Still nothing.

He could hear more people talking into their mobile phones. Serious conversations.

'I'm fine, love. I'm safe.'

'Nobody knows who it is. We're trying to find out.'

'Tell the kids goodnight.'

Matt felt a wave of emotion. His eyes felt hot. He rubbed them. That feeling of helpless anger was coming again.

He punched the phone, leaving the receiver dangling. Then smashed the receiver against the wall, breaking it.

He turned, expecting some reaction from someone. But no one had even noticed.

Because suddenly dozens of men were on the move, walking quickly to the departure gates.

He glanced at the departures board.

His flight. It was leaving.

He started to run.

There was no way he was going to miss this flight.

He wanted to go home.

**What do you think?**

Who do you think is dead?

How is the mood different from what it was on the flight out?

Why does Matt feel 'helpless anger'?

# 11

## *Messages*

———✦———

Matt switched his phone on as he walked off the plane. He would call Sarah and Grace as soon as he was through arrivals.

He was desperate to talk to them.

On the plane things became clearer.

One confirmed dead.

No name.

Not yet.

But there were rumours. Fenn and Sicky were on another plane. They'd been spotted.

But no one had seen Andy. No one had been able to contact him. Someone had seen him fighting with the Turkish fans, who had been carrying knives.

Matt shook his head. This was unreal.

There was no way Andy was dead.

Dozens of men and a few women walked off the plane and towards arrivals in silence. Not a word said, through passport control, through baggage claim, through customs.

No one was stopped.

No one made eye contact.

But that changed in the arrivals hall.

Several fans had families waiting for them. Unexpected. There were cries and shouts and laughter.

TV cameras caught it all.

Matt felt his phone buzz in his pocket as they walked out to flashbulbs and men with notebooks shouting questions. There were dozens of them. Others with microphones were sidling up to some of the lads as they walked through the arrivals hall.

Matt was desperate to talk to his girls. But not here. Not with all this noise.

Fenn and Sicky were in the arrivals hall waiting for Matt.

Still no words.

They just glanced at each other, then walked towards the car park.

While Fenn was paying for his parking ticket, Matt chose the moment.

He had messages.

*Message received today at 6.45 a.m.*

'Daddy? Are you there? Daddy. I got up early to find you but you were still not there so I put the telly on to see if we won and they said that . . . said that . . . Daddy, answer the phone.'

*Message received at 6.49 a.m.*

'Matt. It's Sarah. Answer your bloody phone . . . Matt . . .'

*Message received at 6.55 a.m.*

'Matt. I've called Fenn's wife. She says he's not answering either. We've heard about . . . you know . . . For God's sake, call me the sec . . . the second you get this . . .'

Now texts were coming through.

'Matt. Text as soon as you land. We're worried. S+G'

Matt ignored the rest of the messages and pressed HOME.

It didn't even ring once.

'Daddy?'

His daughter's voice sounded high-pitched.

'Grace?'

Matt was so happy to hear her.

She was crying now. 'Da . . . Da . . . Daddy . . .'

Then silence.

Voices in the background.

Sarah.

Grace crying.

Other voices.

'Matt?'

'Sarah. I'm OK.'

'Good,' she said in a calm voice. But then she was screaming down the phone. 'It's great that you're OK because we're not OK! We've been going out of our minds . . .'

Fenn and Sicky stood looking the other way as Matt was on the phone.

When Matt finished the call he slipped the phone into his pocket.

It was too much.

'Toilet,' he stuttered.

Fenn nodded and looked away again.

Matt made a dash for the toilets. He was sobbing before he got into the cubicle.

In the car leaving the airport, Fenn got a text.

He checked it as he accelerated on to the motorway.

'It was Andy,' Fenn said in a grave voice.

No one else spoke for the remainder of the journey.

**What do you think?**

Why are Sarah and Grace so worried?

Why is Matt upset?

Why don't they say anything on the way home?

# 12

## *The old man*

———•◦•———

Matt walked up the path, rehearsing what he was going to say to Grace.

*I love you.*

*I'm sorry you were worried.*

*I'm home.*

He could barely think the words, let alone say them, because he felt so emotional. He had to pull himself together.

But he knew that, really, there would be no need for words. Matt just needed to hug his daughter. That was all.

The front door opened as Matt approached his house. A figure was standing in the doorway.

His father-in-law.

Matt's mood shifted from love to hate.

This idiot was in his way.

'You're a bloody disgrace,' shouted his father-in-law. 'What you've put these girls through.'

'Dad.' He could hear Sarah's voice. 'Leave it.'

Matt ignored his father-in-law and pushed past him through the door, wanting to see Sarah and Grace.

As he did, he felt a hand on his shoulder. His father-in-law again.

Matt turned, wanting to punch him. At last, after all these years, he had a good reason to strike out. He drew his arm back.

'Daddy?'

Grace's voice was like a clear bell, bringing him back to his senses.

Matt closed his eyes, dismissing his father-in-law's glare, turned and knelt down on the floor. His daughter ran towards him across the hall.

'Grace,' said Matt, his voice wobbling.

Then she was in his arms. And her arms were round his neck. He felt better now. He felt good, even.

And now Sarah's hand was on his shoulder. Matt looked up at her. He was afraid of how she would be with him. But although her face was lined with worry, she was smiling.

He mouthed 'I'm sorry' to her.

And she smiled again.

And then he saw his in-laws in the open doorway. His mother-in-law had her hands on his father-in-law's chest, holding him back.

But now Matt had eye contact with his father-in-law, everything was about to change. He knew it.

'Daddy.' Grace's voice. 'Don't go away again. Please don't go away again.'

And Matt was ready to make a promise to his daughter. That he would never put her through that again. Never.

'I just don't understand you, Matthew,' the old man interrupted.

'Dad. Leave it.'

'I'll not leave it. I've got my piece to say.'

Matt looked up hard at his father-in-law. A secret, dark look that no one else could see and that was full of violence.

But that did not put the older man off.

'You're a father, Matthew. And you go gallivanting off to these places. And we all sit at home worrying about you. Look at your daughter.'

Matt felt Grace's arms grip tighter round his neck. So tight it hurt.

'She has been going out of her mind,' he went on. 'So has our Sarah. You're a disgrace as a husband and father.'

All the time his father-in-law was going on, Grace was whispering into his ear: 'I love you Daddy, I love you Daddy, I love you Daddy.'

Matt closed his eyes.

He wanted to stay in his daughter's arms.

He wanted to wipe his father-in-law off the face of the earth.

He wanted to see his wife smile again and to know she was OK with him.

Then Grace spoke.

'Who died?' she asked.

Matt gently eased her away from him and looked into her eyes.

'He was called Andy, love,' said Matt. 'You didn't . . .'

Matt's voice broke. He found he couldn't speak. He felt like he was about to collapse. He put his hand out, leaning against the wall.

Andy was dead.

Was it real? Was he really dead?

**What do you think?**

Why does the old man think that Matt is a 'disgrace'? Do you agree?

Why does Grace make him feel better?

What is important to Sarah?

'Matt turned, wanting to punch him.' What would have happened if Matt had given in to this urge, and hit his father-in-law?

# 13

## *Before the funeral*

---

Matt was sitting in his suit when Grace came down for breakfast. He had been up for two hours already, unable to sleep.

Grace was already in her school uniform.

She had been putting it on herself this term. Now that she had moved up to an older class at school she wanted to do some things without help from Matt or Sarah.

His daughter looked at him for a couple of seconds.

'Are you going to Andy's funeral today?' she asked.

'I am, honey.'

Grace paused.

Matt knew that she was thinking about what to say next. It was funny. Weren't children supposed to just say what came into their heads?

'Do you feel sad?' Grace asked, finally.

Matt smiled. 'I do, love.'

'Will you be OK?' she asked.

'I'll be fine,' Matt said.

But he didn't feel fine. Every day since they'd come back from Turkey he had cried. But only on his own. And usually at night, when Grace and Sarah were asleep. They didn't need to see him crying. No one did. Then he could pretend it wasn't really happening.

Matt was aware that his daughter was looking at him. He could see that she was trying to work something out.

'Do you want me to come to the funeral with you?' Grace asked. 'I could look after you.'

That was too much for Matt. The pressure in his head felt like an explosion.

'I'd better go,' he said, trying to sound calm.

But he could tell from the look on Grace's face that he didn't look calm.

'OK, Daddy,' she said.

**What do you think?**

Matt tells Grace that he is OK. What makes you think he is not OK?

What do you think would happen if Matt told Sarah how he feels?

Why is what Grace says 'too much for Matt'?

# 14

## Andy's funeral

It rained throughout the funeral. Matt could hear the water hitting the outside of the stained glass windows. He hoped it would stop before they went outside.

The vicar apologized for the dripping sound. It was a leak in the roof. Someone had stolen some lead off the church over the weekend, he said.

Matt saw several people shake their heads. The lady sitting next to him said, 'Who would do something like that?'

Matt shrugged.

The funeral was miserable. Andy's family were huddled at the front, all in black, their shoulders hunched. Like a row of rooks in a storm. Matt tried to work out who was who.

The old bald guy. That was Andy's dad.

The woman with huge bags under her eyes. The one who couldn't stop crying. That was his mum.

The two good-looking women. His sisters. Matt had met one of them once. They'd got off with each other. But he wasn't sure which one.

Thoughts like that kept coming into Matt's head. Thoughts he didn't want to think. Not at a funeral.

The time he'd punched Andy at a service station on the way back from Chelsea. Because Andy had nicked his burger.

The time him and Andy had been arrested together on a stag do in Blackpool. They'd spent five hours in a freezing cell. Just the two of them. They'd talked that night. Matt couldn't remember what they'd talked about, but it had been good.

Andy had never had many girlfriends, Matt thought. No wife now. No kids. The next thought that passed through Matt's mind was that that was a good thing. At least he hadn't left kids behind.

Matt closed his eyes and put his head down.

Imagine that. Imagine Grace growing up without a dad.

Matt decided to walk home from the funeral.

It was still raining, but he was soaked already. It had been raining when they had gathered round the grave in the churchyard too. Matt had stood with Fenn and some of the other lads, slightly away from Andy's family.

He walked slowly, staring at the ground.

**What do you think?**

How does Matt feel, seeing Andy's family?

In what ways do you think Andy was a good friend?

Why does Matt think about Grace at the funeral?

# 15

## *The promise*

———•◆•———

Matt did Grace's bedtime the night following the funeral.

They lay together on the little IKEA bed that he had constructed, surrounded by pink walls that he had painted. She was wearing the Disney Princess nightdress that she had begged for and that Sarah had ordered for her off the internet.

Matt had planned to read with her, as usual.

But Grace didn't want to read. She said she wanted to ask questions about funerals.

First question. 'What happens at a funeral?'

Matt paused and thought of how he should answer her. Honestly. That was the best thing. He'd learned that.

'There's a church service,' explained Matt, 'where everyone prays and sings and says nice things about the person who died. Then they carry the coffin outside . . .'

'Is the person really in the coffin?' asked Grace. 'Or is it pretend?'

'It's real, honey,' replied Matt. 'Six people carry the coffin and then it's lowered into the grave.'

'Then they bury it?'

'After a few more words. Prayers. Stuff like that.'

'Did anyone cry?'

'Yes,' said Matt. 'Lots of people cry at funerals.'

'Did *you* cry?'

'No.'

'Why not?'

Matt smiled. Grace was asking some good questions. He liked to hear her like this. She was exploring the world. And it was his duty to help her explore it.

He could cope with this.

'I don't know,' he answered. 'I really don't know.'

'Weren't you sad?'

'Yes, I was sad.'

'You cried when you came home from Turkey, Daddy. When you heard about your friend dying.'

'I did,' explained Matt. 'But I cried because *you* were upset.'

'Me?' Grace looked pleased.

'Yes, you. If you're sad, then I'm sad.'

'But that means,' Grace went on, 'you were more sad because I was sad, than because he was dead.'

Matt nodded. She was right. 'I was,' he said.

Matt felt good. He loved it when he had conversations with his daughter like this. When he could be honest. He liked it because he could tell that she knew he was telling the truth.

'Daddy?'

'Yes?'

'Will you make me a promise?'

'Yes,' said Matt, hesitating. 'If I can.'

'Will you promise me that you'll never go to watch the football in Europe again?'

Matt looked down at the floor. Then he closed his eyes. It was a big ask.

'Daddy?'

When he opened his eyes his daughter was still there, still wearing her Disney Princess nightdress. So were the pink walls and the IKEA bed. All there.

There was only one answer Matt could give.

'Yes, honey,' he said. 'I promise.'

**What do you think?**

Why didn't Matt cry at the funeral?

Why does Matt enjoy talking to his daughter?

Is Matt right to make his promise? Why?

# 16

## *Barcelona away*

———————•◦•———————

Sunday afternoon in the pub. And it was half-time in the TV match.

Chelsea v. Stoke.

Outside it was raining heavily, so the smokers were in the doorway, their fumes wafting into the pub. Matt inhaled. It smelt good, like pubs used to smell.

Matt was taking it easy today, drinking bottles of lager instead of pints. He was taking it easy because he knew that, now it was half-time, he had a problem. And that he needed to be sharp to deal with it.

Any minute now, Fenn would be round with his notebook and wallet, gathering names and cash for the Barcelona trip.

The next away game in Europe was the big one. The Spanish champions. Several of the lads had opted out of Istanbul so that they'd be able to afford Barcelona. It was going to be a three-day trip.

And here was Fenn. Dead on time.

'Matt. Three hundred quid. Two nights and the flights. Have you got it on you?'

'No,' said Matt.

'I need it for tomorrow. Can you nip to a cashpoint at the end of the match?'

'I'm not coming,' said Matt.

'Eh?'

'I can't come.'

'Why, mate?' asked Fenn. 'What's up? This is the big one. The one we've been planning for years. The biggest game.'

Matt shrugged, then took a long drink of his lager. He was aware that it was not just Fenn looking at him now. Other lads were listening in, stopping their own conversations.

'His missus won't let him,' said Sicky.

Matt glared at Sicky. If there was one person he couldn't take shit from, it was Sicky.

'Like hell she won't,' said Matt. 'What do you bloody know?'

'Well, what is it, then?' asked Sicky. 'Are you scared?'

Matt shook his head and stood up, his eyes fixed on Sicky. He could feel that all the blood in his body had rushed to his head. A thick, thumping ache building.

Sicky stepped back.

Matt felt the pressure building across his back and arms. That Incredible Hulk feeling again. Was this the moment he could finally smack Sicky, the moment he had dreamed of for months? And if he couldn't get away with smacking his father-in-law, then he could easily get away with punching Sicky.

'Seriously,' interrupted Fenn. 'What is it?'

'I'm skint,' lied Matt.

'Skint? You've been doing more work than ever. You must be loaded.'

'It's stuff at home,' said Matt.

Ten or more of the lads were looking at Matt now, seeing he was squirming. Matt could feel his face going pink. His eyes felt hot.

And all he could think of was Grace. Of lying on Grace's bed and saying that he would never go away in Europe again. Of his promise.

Sicky stepped forward again, sensing that Matt was on the back foot now.

'He's scared,' Sicky said to Fenn.

Fenn was looking at Matt with a different look on his face, like he was asking a question.

Matt closed his eyes, then lunged at Sicky, his fist hitting the younger lad's cheekbone.

Immediately Matt was pulled back by two or three lads behind him. And Sicky had turned his back on the fight, holding his cheek.

'What the hell was that for?' Fenn asked Matt.

'He's had it coming.'

Matt felt full of power.

Sicky was backing off, picking up his drink now, not wanting to fight.

Matt had won.

And he could see that Fenn was smiling.

'Maybe he is a meathead,' said Fenn. 'Maybe. But when can you get me the money for Barcelona?'

It was something to do with Fenn smiling that made Matt change his mind. Fenn was the top lad. Fenn, in smiling, had told Matt that he thought he'd done a good thing in putting Sicky in his place.

'OK,' said Matt, his hand already in his pocket. 'I'll give you it now.'

**What do you think?**

Why is Matt unable to tell his mates the real reason he can't go?

Why does Matt say that Sicky 'had it coming'? Do you agree?

Why does Matt feel 'full of power' after hitting him?

What makes Matt pay up and decide to go to Barcelona?

# 17

## *The library*

---•◦•---

Monday. Two weeks later. A beautiful sunny evening.

Matt waited in the school playground with the other parents. A couple of mums smiled at him and he smiled back. He recognized them from parties he had taken Grace to.

Matt wished that he was more confident and could go up to the other parents and talk to them, but he always felt shy at the school gates. He always felt that he didn't belong there. Or that he wasn't good enough to be there. Even that they might think he was a paedophile. Something like that.

Grace ran across the playground and flung herself into his arms.

'How was school?' asked Matt.

'Fine.'

'What did you do?'

'Lots of things.'

Matt tried to find out more about Grace's day at school as they walked hand in hand along the High Street.

'Can we go to the library, please, Daddy?'

'Yes, honey.'

They waited at the zebra crossing for a bus to stop, then walked across the road.

'I wish you weren't going to London,' said Grace, as they approached the library.

Matt winced.

'Me too,' he said.

Matt had made up a story that he was working in London for a week, so that he could go to Spain and watch the Barcelona game. He'd worked away in London before, so it didn't sound unusual.

'I'll miss you,' said Grace, skipping alongside him, her hand still in his.

'I'll miss you too,' replied Matt. 'But we need the money.'

Matt led Grace into the library, wondering why he was adding to his lie.

He felt ashamed that most of the things he was saying to his daughter were untrue, and as she ran to the children's book section he felt lonely.

'Hello, Mr Baird,' one of the librarians called out. 'Hello, Grace.'

Matt said hello. Grace was already taking books off the shelves.

Then Matt heard the librarians. 'He's a great dad,' one of them said. 'He always brings young Grace here. I wish all the dads were like him.'

The library was a long, thin building with bookshelves running along each wall. There were computers and CDs and DVDs on stands.

At the far end of the library, the children's section was decorated with pictures of favourite children's characters, like Pooh Bear and Peter Rabbit.

Matt leaned against one of the tables. He was feeling sick.

Overhearing the librarians saying that he was a good dad had reminded him of what his father-in-law had said when he had come back from Istanbul.

*You're a disgrace as a husband and father.*

That was what was making him feel sick. His father-in-law had been right. That stupid, competitive old man was right about Matt. He was going to Spain. He was going to break his promise. He *was* a disgrace.

'Daddy, look at me.'

Grace was coming over to Matt. Her arms were loaded with large hardback books.

Matt helped her to put them down.

'I've found all these books about different countries. Like the book about Turkey. If we read these together you won't have to go away any more. We can find out about the places in books.'

Matt forced a laugh and looked at the book on top of the pile.

The book was called *Tell Me About Spain.*

Matt stopped laughing.

**What do you think?**

What do you think of Matt's story, about work in London?

Matt said earlier that he liked being honest with his daughter. How does lying to her make him feel?

What makes the librarians think that Matt is a 'great dad'? Do you agree?

How do you think Matt feels when he sees the book about Spain?

# 18

## *Passport*

---

Matt woke at five in the morning. Time to go to Barcelona.

He slipped slowly out of bed, desperate not to wake Sarah and Grace.

Grace had been in their bed with them for a few days. She sometimes did, usually when something was worrying her at school.

It was cold in the house. The central heating had not kicked in yet. Matt wanted to get back into bed and go back to sleep to the sound of his wife and daughter breathing.

But Fenn would be outside the library in half an hour. With Sicky. Ready for the drive to the airport. He had to be there. If he wasn't, he'd never hear the last of it.

Matt washed his face and brushed his teeth in the kitchen downstairs. He didn't want to create noise in the house. But it wasn't like he was creeping out on them. They knew he'd be going off while they were still asleep. That wasn't a lie.

The lie was that they thought he was going to London to work, not to Barcelona to watch football.

Matt pressed the sides of his head. He had to stop thinking. Just get his stuff and go. It was simple.

Sarah had packed Matt's rucksack the night before. Clothes. Bathroom stuff. His wallet. Everything he would need for a week working in London.

But Matt needed one more thing.

His passport.

How stupid was he? Why had he not got the passport last night, when Sarah and Grace were downstairs in the kitchen? Now he had to go back into the bedroom and find it in the box on top of the wardrobe. In the dark.

He crept back upstairs and into the bedroom, wary of waking his wife and daughter.

Matt stood on a stool and eased the box down.

Suddenly he felt something slide off the top of the box and hit the floor.

Matt froze. He stopped breathing.

A pile of letters had fallen and had scattered. Both Sarah and Grace shifted in the bed. If one of them opened their eyes now he'd be busted.

But, to Matt's great relief, they both settled and the room was still and silent.

Slowly and carefully, he gathered the letters and put them on top of the box.

Now he was late.

**What do you think?**

What could be worrying Grace?

How does Sarah support Matt?

Why is Matt going to Barcelona? Do you think he is right to go?

# 19

## *Dead like Andy?*

Five minutes later Matt was walking down his street. He had a rucksack over his shoulder and a passport in his pocket.

It was a strange morning. A huge bank of dark grey cloud filled half the sky. A cold wind was driving in from the north. This was not what the weather forecast had predicted.

Matt knew he had to rush. Fenn would draw up in his car by the library in five minutes.

He couldn't be late. Not for Barcelona away. This was the big one. The greatest fixture you could see your football club play.

Matt grinned and quickened his pace. Along the road. Left at the postbox. Past Grace's school.

Matt slowed slightly.

Grace's school. The playground. The mural on the wall. The brightly painted doors and windows. By the time Sarah and Grace arrived here in three hours, Matt would be sitting on a plane about to take off to Spain.

Matt turned his mind to three days of drinking, messing about and going to one of the greatest football stadiums in the world. Better to think about the joys that lay ahead, not the problems he was leaving behind at home.

But he could not turn his mind.

All he could think about was that he was breaking his promise to his daughter. The promise he had made because she was afraid he would end up like Andy.

Dead like Andy.

*You'll have to be stronger than this*, he told himself. *You will have to toughen up.*

If Fenn – and especially Sicky – got a whiff of how he was feeling, they'd rip him apart.

And that was what made his mind up.

The thought of Sicky having that over him stirred an anger inside him. An anger that he could use to try to forget his daughter.

When Matt saw Fenn's blue and battered VW Golf in front of the library, it crossed his mind that he should just text Fenn and say he was not going to Barcelona.

But that wasn't an option.

Not really.

Was it?

Matt jogged across the road and looked into the car through the passenger window. Sicky was in the front seat and just stared blankly at Matt.

Matt wondered whether Sicky was disappointed to see him. Maybe Sicky thought that Matt wasn't going to turn up. Maybe he thought that Matt was too soft on his family now, not one of the lads.

The thought brought a smile to Matt's face.

Unlike Sicky, Fenn looked happy to see Matt. Really happy.

'Matty. Jump in. Climb aboard the three-days-of-fun train, my friend.'

Matt leaned on the roof of the car and looked in. First at Sicky. Then at Fenn.

'I'm sorry, Fenn. I'm not coming,' he heard himself say.

'What?' asked Fenn.

Matt saw a smile creeping across Sicky's face.

'I'm sorry I've brought you out of your way. Really sorry. But I've decided that I'm not coming to Barcelona.'

'Why the hell not?' Fenn spat.

Matt swallowed.

'I promised Grace I wouldn't go to an away game again,' he explained. 'After Istanbul.'

Matt walked home. Over the main road. Past Grace's school. Past the postbox and right at the end of the road.

The dark mass of cloud was clearing and he found himself looking forward to two more hours in bed with his family before he would get up and walk Grace to school.

### What do you think?

How does Matt 'use' his anger, and is it a good way to handle the situation?

How will Matt explain to Sarah and Grace that he hasn't gone to London?

Why do you think he decides not to go? Is it the right decision?

Do you think he will still go to the pub with Fenn?